Maniac Magee

Grades 4-6

Written by Ron Leduc
Illustrated by Sean Parkes

ISBN 1-55035-550-3
Copyright 1998
Revised December 2005
All Rights Reserved * Printed in Canada

Published in the United States by:
On the Mark Press
3909 Witmer Road PMB 175
Niagara Falls, New York
14305
www.onthemarkpress.com

Published in Canada by:
S&S Learning Materials
15 Dairy Avenue
Napanee, Ontario
K7R 1M4
www.sslearning.com

Look For Other Junior - Novel Studies

Charlotte's Web .... Gr 4-6
Little House in the Big Woods 4-6
Owls In The Family 4-6
Underground to Canada 4-6
The Lion, The Witch and The Wardrobe 4-6
Tales of a Fourth Grade Nothing 4-6
Trumpet of the Swan 4-6
On the Banks of Plum Creek 4-6
Pippi Longstocking 4-6
Bridge to Terabithia 4-6
The Secret Garden 4-6
James and the Giant Peach 4-6
Charlie and the Chocolate Factory 4-6
Chocolate Fever 4-6
Wayside School is Falling Down 4-6
There's a Boy in the Girl's Bathroom 4-6
Abel's Island 4-6
Mr. Popper's Penguins 4-6
Mouse and the Motorcycle 4-6
Pinballs 4-6
Indian in the Cupboard 4-6
Sadako and the 1000 Paper Cranes 4-6
Return of the Indian 4-6
Best Christmas Pageant Ever 4-6
Harriet the Spy 4-6
How to Eat Fried Worms 4-6
Stone Fox 4-6
Castle in the Attic 4-6
Shiloh 4-6
Summer of the Swans 4-6
Maniac Magee 4-6
The Great Gilly Hopkins 4-6
King of the Wind 4-6
The Incredible Journey 4-6
Dear Mr. Henshaw 4-6
Midnight Fox 4-6
The Door in the Wall 4-6
BFG 4-6
The Whipping Boy 4-6
A Taste of Blackberries 4-6
The Family Under the Bridge 4-6
Bunnicula 4-6
The War with Grandpa 4-6
Radio Fifth Grade 4-6
Little House on the Prairie 4-6
Chocolate Touch 4-6
Midwife's Apprentice 4-6
Number the Stars 4-6
Holes 4-6
Reading With Kenneth Oppel 4-6
The Egypt Game 4-6

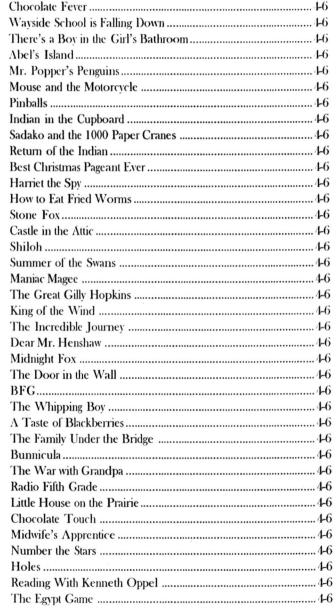

Table of Contents

Expectations 4

Summary of Story 4

Author Biography 5

Other Books by Jerry Spinelli 5

Teacher Tips 6

Features of the Program 7

List of Skills 7

Cover Page for the Booklet 8

Just the Facts 9

Chapter Activities 10

Blank Activity Sheet 57

Answer Key 58

MANIAC MAGEE

by Jerry Spinelli

Expectations

The students will:

- implement major strategies used during the reading process.
- practice and reinforce a variety of language skills.
- develop a love for reading.
- improve and develop their creativity.
- will have their work assessed through the use of a novel as a teaching tool.

Story Summary

Maniac Magee was born in Bridgeport. His parents were killed when the trolley on which they rode crashed into the Schuylkill River. He went to live with his Aunt Dot and Uncle Dan. When he could no longer stand living there, he ran away and became a homeless person at the age of eleven. A legend named Maniac (born Jeffrey Lionel Magee) began as he ran back 200 miles to the town of Two Mills which is right across the Schuylkill River from Bridgeport. Maniac earned his name through his extraordinary running speed, his abrupt unexpected appearances and his talent both in catching footballs and hitting baseballs.

The first person to actually stop and talk to Maniac was Amanda Beale. She lived in the East End, a black neighborhood. Other people along the way were: James "Hands" Down, a football player, Arnold Jones, a Finsterwallies candidate, the Pickwells, a large family, John McNab, a Little League pitcher and Mars Bar, the baddest kid in town.

Amanda invites Maniac to her home to meet the rest of the family. When Mr. Beale realizes Maniac is homeless, he "adopts" him. Maniac loves his new home and the color of the East End. But everyone and everything did not love him back. When he read the tall yellow letters, "ISHBELLY GO HOME", Maniac left the East End. Rather than creating problems for the Beales, Maniac walked out of town.

His new home was the buffalo pen at Elmwood Park. Here he is befriended by Grayson, a park maintenance worker. Grayson invites Maniac to stay with him at Two Mills Y.M.C.A. Maniac, in turn, helps Grayson around the zoo, putting up fences, hauling stones and other jobs. This relationship blossoms and the two stay together for several months. Maniac teaches Grayson how to read while Grayson teaches Maniac baseball techniques and refinements. This happy home life ends with Grayson's abrupt death. Maniac is again homeless.

The McNab family take Maniac in. The legend of Maniac grows as he performs a number of heroic feats. Then one day he is issued the most perilous challenge of all: to go into the East End. The East End - West End, black and white situation did not bother Maniac. It was rather the racial tension and the trouble it might cause for everyone. The final strain was a birthday party at the McNabs and a game called "Rebel". In this game, the whites were in the pillbox and the blacks were outside. Rather than condone this situation, Maniac started to run. He ran back to the buffalo pen at the zoo.

Mars Bar visits Maniac and invites him to his home. Despite his pleading, Maniac remains firm in his decision to stay in the buffalo pen. The next visitor is Amanda Beale who insists Maniac go home with her. Her persistence wins, and Maniac leaves the zoo. He knew that finally someone was calling him home.

Author Biography

Born February 1,1941, in Norristown P.A., he was educated at Gettysberg College, Johns Hopkins University and Temple University. He served as U.S. Naval Reserve from 1966 to 1972. He received the Boston Globe/Horn Book Award, the Newbery Medal, D. C. Fisher Award, Pacific Northwest Readers' Choice Award - all for Maniac Magee. He also received the Carolyn Field Award; the South Carolina Children's Book Award and the California Young Reader Medal in 1993.

His style and content is appealing to young adults, particularly those facing social, moral and personal problems, just like those of his characters. Real life experience and events form the basis of his novels. He says, "When I write a book you can think of it as my way of telling you what I saw and felt, feared, wished, imagined and remembered on the way to school." Spinelli has the ability to bring even the most remote setting or situation to life.

Spinelli is noted as a teller of adolescent tales as he recreates the teenage years with accuracy and humor. He covers such controversial topics as racism and sex in his stories.

Other Books by Jerry Spinelli

Space Station Seventh Grade

Night of the Whale

The Bathwater Gang

There's a Girl in My Hammerlock

Do the Funky Pickle

Jason and Marceline

The Bathwater Gang Gets Down to Business

Dump Days

Who Put That Hair in My Toothbrush?

Picklemania

Fourth Grade Rats

School Daze: Report to the Principals Office

Who Ran My Underwear Up the Flagpole

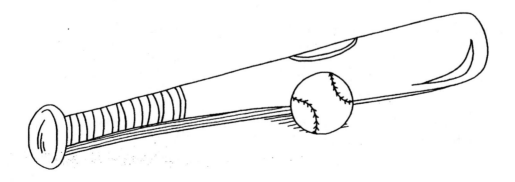

MANIAC MAGEE

by Jerry Spinelli

Tips For Teachers

At last... A teacher-friendly visual Language Arts approach to novel study. A novel study that is complete with answers, suggested responses, and related activities that are compatible with any curriculum.

The novel could be read in a variety of ways - the teacher may choose to read a chapter, have the children read to each other, or have them read silently.

Reading is an act of creation. It requires a translation of words into visual images. In each chapter, children are asked to interpret the text and to present information by drawing. The use of labels would enhance some drawings. This activity could be done individually or collaboratively. This creative and critical-thinking activity would make an attractive montage or bulletin-board display.

The chapter questions should be previewed and discussed before reading. Questions using "Do you think..." are open-ended and could be completed individually or in a small group setting.

The major strategies of reading are emphasized throughout the unit. Each chapter should have a title. That title would be the main idea of the section. Sequencing activities are prevalent in the unit. True/False questions require comprehension and interpretation of the text.

Extensive practise in language forms and conventions reinforce good punctuation and language usage. Students should respond to most questions in sentence form. Different activities highlight punctuation, spelling, grammar, language structures, and patterns.

Collaborative tasks require group work and group decision-making skills. The talking, listening, and discussing components of language are utilized. Some tasks could be to predict outcomes or to decide on particular features of an illustration.

CLOZE activities require children to select appropriate words to fit in a certain context. The author's choice could be found before or after this activity.

Synonyms, antonyms, and word definition activities aid in vocabulary development.

Favorite scenes or chapters could be developed into skits. These, in turn, could be further communicated in video performances. The videos are a normal evolution from the artist's interpretations of each chapter.

Assessment makes this novel study teacher-friendly. The answer key follows the same format as the student book. The learning outcomes are easily identifiable. Suggested answers are given for inference questions. Although it is important to assess children's work, the novel study is meant to be a teaching tool. It is extremely important to review the work and to discuss the answers. Assignments may be teacher evaluated, peer evaluated, or self evaluated.

The completed unit is a valuable reference for parent interviews. When all is said and done, the major objective of the novel study is to foster a love for reading.

Features of the Program

- Compatible with any curriculum.
- Visualization.
- Variety of reading techniques.
- Uses major strategies of reading.
- Identifies main ideas.
- Practise in language forms and conventions.
- Individual or collaborative activities.
- CLOZE exercises.
- Variety of evaluation techniques.
- Identifiable learning outcomes.
- Ease of assessment and parental reporting.

Skills Featured in the Unit

Learning outcomes emphasized in the unit.

Adjectives	Alliteration	Alphabetical Order
Brainstorming	Cloze	Commas
Chants	Contraction	Clichés
Definitions	Homonyms	Metric Math
Geometry	Prepositions	Phrases
Plurals	Punctuation	Prefixes
Quotations	Hink Pinks	Menu Design
Sentences	Sequence	Simile
Spelling	Parallelism	Vowels
Consonants	Numerical Order	Word Puzzles
Scrambled Words	Word Association	Word Usage
Words within Words	Word Games	Guide Words

MANIAC MAGEE

by Jerry Spinelli

Name: _____

OTM-14160 • SSN1-160 Maniac Magee

by Jerry Spinelli

Just the Facts

1. Title of the Book: _____

2. Author: _____

3. Book Award: _____

   _____

   _____

4. Main Character:

   a) _____

   b) _____

   c) _____

   d) _____

   e) _____

5. Publisher: _____

6. Countries of Publication: _____

7. Dedicated to: _____

8. Main Character: _____

9. Story Location: _____

10. ISBN #: _____

by Jerry Spinelli

Chapters 1 and 2 - Title:_____ Page 1

Illustrate the answers to these statements.

1. Maniac Magee was born here.	**2.** What happened to his parents.
3. What Maniac sang in the musical.	**4.** How far Maniac ran.
5. How many people claimed to have seen him that first day.	**6.** Maniac passing a stranger.

MANIAC MAGEE

by Jerry Spinelli

A) What was Maniac's real name?

_____

_____

_____

B) Where did he go to live after his parents died?

_____

_____

_____

C) Why do you think Maniac leaves his relatives?

_____

_____

_____

D) Where did Maniac wind up?

_____

_____

_____

E) Make up a skipping chant of six to eight lines. Try to have consecutive lines rhyme.

_____

_____

_____

_____

_____

_____

_____

F) Punctuate the following.

1. little jeffrey was shipped off to his Nearest relatives aunt dot and uncle dan

_____

_____

2. as he passed them he said hi

_____

_____

3. they lived in holidaysburg in the western part of pennsylvania

_____

_____

4. two mills is right across the schuylkill river from bridgeport

_____

_____

5. the song they sang was talk to the animals

_____

_____

MANIAC MAGEE

by Jerry Spinelli

Chapters 3 and 4 - Title: _____ Page 3

A) **Illustrate** the contents of Amanda Beale's suitcase.

B) **Sketch** an overhead view of the football field. **Identify** key players. Use arrows to Show direction of the thrown football and the run by Maniac.

MANIAC MAGEE

by Jerry Spinelli

A) How was the town divided?

_____

_____

_____

B) Why can't Jeffrey return Amanda's book?

_____

_____

C) Create your own similes.

1. flapping like _____

_____

2. as smooth as _____

_____

3. eyes as blue as _____

_____

4. as hot as _____

_____

5. complexion dark like _____

_____

6. as fast as _____

_____

7. stunned like _____

8. as hungry as _____

_____

9. as thirsty _____

10. house looked like _____

_____

D) What were the other **two** appearances that first day?

_____

_____

_____

_____

E) What was unusual about the way the kid had done everything?

_____

_____

_____

_____

F) Suffixes

1. friend + ly = _____
2. reduce + ing = _____
3. slam + ed = _____
4. hesitate + ed = _____
5. true + ly = _____
6. stare + ed = _____
7. take + ing = _____
8. carry + ed = _____
9. rip + ed = _____
10. weave + ing = _____
11. stun + ed = _____
12. argue + ment = _____
13. drop + ing = _____
14. beg + ing = _____
15. fat + er = _____

Chapters 5 and 6 - Title:_____ Page 5

A) **Sketch** and **name** things found in Finsterwald's backyard.

C) **Draw** an overhead view to show what the kid was running on.

B) This is the dinner table at the Pickwells. **Identify** everyone sitting around the table. You may have to make up names for some people.

MANIAC MAGEE

by Jerry Spinelli

A) What are the "finsterwallies" and how do you get them?

_____

_____

_____

_____

B) What happened to Arnold Jones at 803 Oriole Street?

_____

_____

_____

_____

C) Fill in the blanks. Add necessary punctuation.

1. The highschoolers were watching the _____ the _____ and the _____.

2. The Pickwell children ran in from the _____ from the _____ from the _____ and from _____.

3. Six things I like to eat are.

____ ____ ____ ____ ____ ____

4. Seven of my favorite names are.

____ ____ ____ ____ ____ ____ ____

5. Two streets in my town are.

____ ____

D) Match words with their definitions.

1. ___ infamous   **A)** a continuous demanding

2. ___ blunder   **B)** an apparent perception

3. ___ mirage   **C)** to look with half closed eyes

4. ___ emanations   **D)** to proceed carelessly

5. ___ hallucinations   **E)** scrutinize closely

6. ___ scan   **F)** an optical illusion

7. ___ squint   **G)** notorious

8. ___ clamor   **H)** outcomes

E) Explain the Pickwell whistle.

_____

_____

_____

F) How did the kid help Arnold Jones?

_____

_____

_____

_____

by *Jerry Spinelli*

A) **Draw** a baseball diamond. **Label** the positions on the playing field. Indicate by a broken line where each of the balls or frog went when Maniac was the batter.

B) This is a birth certificate. Indicate what information should be on it. **Fill out** the information about you.

MANIAC MAGEE

by Jerry Spinelli

A) Fill in the blanks with suitable words. Find the author's choice (A.C.)

1. There was only one pitch he ever threw:
   _____ _____
   _____ _____
   (A.C.) _____

2. McNab croaked from the mound, "Get outta there,
   _____ _____
   _____ _____
   (A.C.) _____

3. When he wasn't reading, he was
   _____ _____
   _____ _____
   (A.C.) _____

4. It wasn't a ball at all, it was a
   _____ _____
   _____ _____
   (A.C.) _____

B) **State** your impression of McNab.

_____
_____
_____

C) How did you feel when you read he had tattooed McNab's fastball?

_____
_____
_____

D) Explain why he was called Maniac.

_____
_____
_____
_____

E) What is the story of "The Children's Crusade"?

_____
_____
_____
_____

F) Find **five** words that begin with the given letter and are still words if the first letter is removed. Most words can be found in the chapters.

First letter "W"

_____ _____
_____ _____
_____ _____
_____ _____

First letter "T"

_____ _____
_____ _____
_____ _____
_____ _____

First letter "S"

_____ _____
_____ _____
_____ _____
_____ _____

Chapters 9 and 10 - Title: _____ Page 9

A) After Maniac left the steel rails he ran past many things. **Draw** and **name** six of them. Keep the places in proper sequence.

1.	2.	3.

4.	5.	6.

B) Illustrate with color and labels several chocolate bars that you like. Show the bar that you think the Thompson boy was eating.

Maniac Magee
by Jerry Spinelli

A) What two conclusions did John McNab come to?

_____

_____

_____

_____

B) Why were the Cobras laughing when they were standing at Hector Street?

_____

_____

_____

C) Whom did Maniac meet in the East End?

_____

_____

D) How was a fight between Mars Bar and Maniac avoided?

_____

_____

_____

_____

E) Why was there dead silence after Maniac took a bite of the candy bar?

_____

_____

_____

_____

F) What is your impression of Mars Bar?

_____

_____

_____

G) Combine these short sentecnes into a longer more interesting sentence.

1. He was down by Red Hill. He was heading away from them. He had his book in his hand.

_____

_____

2. Once he wobbled. He leaped from the rail to the ground. Then he took off.

_____

_____

3. Now and then people crossed the line. They crossed it if they were adults. They crossed it in daylight.

_____

_____

4. The kid hadn't even gone for the unused end. He had chomped right over Mars Bar's own bite marks.

_____

_____

MANIAC MAGEE

by Jerry Spinelli

Chapters 11 and 12 - Title: _____ Page 11

A) Amanada claimed that it was one of her favorite pages that was ripped out. **Sketch** two pages from your favorite books.

B) **Illustrate** the scene in the kitchen with Hester and Lester.

MANIAC MAGEE

by Jerry Spinelli

A) How was Maniac saved from a confrontation with Mars Bar?

_____

_____

_____

_____

B) How did Amanda see the torn page of the book?

_____

_____

_____

C) Fill in the blanks using the example as a guide.

Adjective	Person	Place	Occupation
Daring	Donald	Detroit	Designer
Awesome	Alf	Alberta	Artist

1. _____ _____ _____ _____
2. _____ _____ _____ _____
3. _____ _____ _____ _____
4. _____ _____ _____ _____
5. _____ _____ _____ _____
6. _____ _____ _____ _____
7. _____ _____ _____ _____
8. _____ _____ _____ _____

D) Write the **contractions** for

1. it is _____   8. was not _____
2. they are _____   9. did not _____
3. who is _____   10. that is _____
4. you are _____   11. what is _____
5. could not _____   12. I am _____
6. we will _____   13. there is _____
7. were not _____   14. do not _____

E) What mistake did Maniac make when Mr. Beale was driving him home?

_____

_____

_____

_____

F) What did Mr. Beale do when Maniac told him he didn't have a home?

_____

_____

_____

_____

MANIAC MAGEE

by Jerry Spinelli

Chapters 13 and 14 - Title: _____

A) I hope you're not allergic to the same thing as Maniac. **Draw** what it was. Label all the ingredients.

B) **Illustrate** the profile of your favorite sneaker.

MANIAC MAGEE
by Jerry Spinelli

Chapters 13 and 14

A) Write sentences to **illustrate** the meanings of these **homonyms**.

1. (hare, hair) _____
   _____
   _____

2. (soar, sore) _____
   _____

3. (you;'re, your) _____
   _____
   _____

4. (who's, whose) _____
   _____
   _____

5. (petal, pedal, peddle) _____
   _____
   _____

B) Tell **five** ways Maniac fitted in.

1. _____
2. _____
3. _____
4. _____
5. _____

C) Tell **five** things that you do at home to help out.

1. _____
2. _____
3. _____
4. _____
5. _____

D) List **five** things Maniac loved in his new life.

1. _____
2. _____
3. _____
4. _____
5. _____

E) What colors were the people of the East End?

1. _____ 2. _____

3. _____ 4. _____

5. _____ 6. _____

7. _____

F) Arrange these words in **numerical** order.

a) bicycle   1. _____
b) quartet   2. _____
c) hexagon   3. _____
d) octopus   4. _____
e) unicorn   5. _____
f) November   6. _____
g) decimal   7. _____
h) pentathlon   8. _____
i) century   9. _____
j) September   10. _____
k) trio   11. _____

MANIAC MAGEE
by Jerry Spinelli

A) Show Hands talking "trash" to Maniac. Let each balloon be a different "trash talk".

B) Write a **recipe** for Mrs. Beale's famous meatloaf.

_____

_____

_____

_____

_____

_____

_____

_____

_____

Maniac Magee

by Jerry Spinelli

A) List **five** things that made Maniac famous.

_____

_____

_____

_____

_____

B) What are some things you will be famous for?

_____

_____

_____

C) Write sentences to show the difference between these sound alike words.

1. (dessert, desert) _____

_____

_____

2. (angel, angle) _____

_____

_____

3. (dairy, diary) _____

_____

_____

4. (picture, pitcher) _____

_____

_____

5. (cloths, clothes) _____

_____

_____

D) What do you think these clichés mean?

1. Take the bull by the horns.

_____

_____

2. pie in the sky

_____

_____

3. rob Peter to pay Paul

_____

_____

4. bark up the wrong tree

_____

_____

5. wrapped up in your work

_____

_____

E) What do you think of Maniac's outlook on life?

_____

_____

_____

_____

F) List **five** things Maniac couldn't see.

_____

_____

_____

_____

_____

Maniac Magee

by Jerry Spinelli

Chapters 17 and 18 - Title: _____ Page 17

A) There are a lot of words associated with fire hydrant. Help your teacher with the word associations. **Pick a word. Create** a word web by writing down as many words as you know that are associations.

B) **Solve** the scrambled words. Use the letters to answer the riddle.

OTO ☐☐ _

TTERUBY ☐ _ _ _ _ ☐ _ _

GNIKOARC ☐ _ ☐ _ ☐ _ ☐ _

ACBKL ☐☐ _ _ _

HESEP ☐ _ _ _ _

What did Amanda tell Jeffrey about?

_ _ _ _ _ _ _ _ _ ' _

_ _ _ _ _

C) **Design** your library card.

Maniac Magee
by Jerry Spinelli

A) Why was the old Ragpicker ranting to Maniac?

_____

_____

_____

_____

B) What was in yellow letters on the Beale's house?

_____

_____

C) State some reasons Amanda gave for Maniac to stay.

_____

_____

_____

_____

_____

D) What do you think Cobble's Knot is all about?

_____

_____

_____

_____

E) What does Amanda say when asked why was she up so late?

How would you reply?

1. _____

2. _____

3. _____

4. _____

5. _____

6. _____

F) A **prepositional phrase** starts with a **preposition** and ends with a **noun**. Using these prepostions, write prepositional phrases.

under the _____

through _____

from a _____

behind _____

toward _____

after _____

above _____

between _____

to _____

below _____

Maniac Magee
by Jerry Spinelli

A) Design a poster that would advertise the Knot challenge.

B) Pretend that you are Mr. Cobble getting ready for the Knot challenge.
Design a menu and prices for this event. Mention foods that are this chapter.

by Jerry Spinelli

Chapters 19 and 20   Page 20

A) Find the word that **matches** the definitions. The circled letters tell you what Mr. Cobble sold.

color of a leaf

a place for contests

a smell

a collection of sheep

not true

a group name for plants

a creature from another place

not light

a smelly carnivore

— — — — — — — —

B) Explain how Cobble's Knot came into existence.

_____

_____

_____

_____

C) Describe Cobble's Knot.

_____

_____

_____

_____

D) What would Maniac need to untangle Cobble's Knot?

_____

_____

_____

_____

E) According to some people, how did Maniac view Cobble's Knot?

_____

_____

_____

_____

F) **Write** sentences using the prepositional phrases from the previous chapter.

1. _____

2. _____

3. _____

4. _____

5. _____

6. _____

7. _____

8. _____

9. _____

10. _____

MANIAC MAGEE
by Jerry Spinelli

Chapter 21 - Title: _____ Page 21

A) This is a sketch of Two Mills. **Show** where Maniac walked and where the Cobras and East Enders were. **Name** the Streets and Avenues.

B) These are words from Amanda's encyclopedia. Put them in **alphabetical order**.

Algebra 1. _____

Auk 2. _____

Ankara 3. _____

Africa 4. _____

Alaska 5. _____

Azores 6. _____

Anzio 7. _____

Apple 8. _____

Amazon 9. _____

Algeria 10. _____

Aristotle 11. _____

Anableps 12. _____

C) **Write** down some autographs you would like to have.

1. _____

2. _____

3. _____

4. _____

5. _____

6. _____

7. _____

8. _____

9. _____

10. _____

Maniac Magee
by Jerry Spinelli

A) A short name can be inserted in each choice below to complete a longer word. Cross off list as you go.

don	hank	ross	art
able	carl	ron	eve
bud	tom	ned	ruth
norm	gene	leo	hal

1. t _ _ _ _ _ s
2. st _ _ _ _ ed
3. ac _ _ _ _ _
4. s _ _ _ _ ach
5. _ _ _ _ _ al
6. t _ _ _ _ _ s
7. _ _ _ _ _ tic
8. s _ _ _ _ _ et

9. f _ _ _ _ t
10. un _ _ _ _ e
11. n _ _ _ _ r
12. _ _ _ _ get
13. t _ _ _ _ _ ful
14. _ _ _ _ pard
15. c _ _ _ _ lenge
16. ear _ _ _ _

B) If each block is 500 meters and each intersection 12.5 meters how long is the string?

_____ meters

_____ kilometers

_____ decimeters

_____ centimeters

_____ millimeters

C) How was the homemade confetti made?

_____

_____

_____

_____

D) Write **three** adjectives to describe each of the following topics.

1. Maniac after unravelling the knot

_____ _____ _____

2. Amanda on examining the confetti

_____ _____ _____

3. Maniac walking north on Hector

_____ _____ _____

4. Mr. Cobble handing the certificate to maniac

_____ _____ _____

5. The people at Cobble's corners

_____ _____ _____

6. Maniac wanting to hug Amanda

_____ _____ _____

7. How you feel about the situation

_____ _____ _____

E) Who destroyed Amanda's encyclopedia?

_____

_____

_____

F) Why did Maniac leave town?

_____

_____

_____

Chapters 22 and 23 - Title: _____ Page 23

A) Illustrate where Grayson found Maniac.

B) Show how many Krimpets Grayson bought.

MANIAC MAGEE

by Jerry Spinelli

A) Who rescued Maniac?

_____

_____

_____

_____

B) Why was Maniac where he was?

_____

_____

C) What was the tiny idea that was worming its way into Grayson's head?

_____

_____

_____

D) Explain Maniac's dislike of school.

_____

_____

_____

_____

_____

E) Put the following events in sequential order.

1. Grayson covers Maniac with his jacket. ___
2. Grayson and Maniac both laugh. ___
3. The baby buffalo watches Maniac on the ground. ___
4. Grayson hoists Maniac into the pickup. ___
5. Maniac falls from the fence. ___
6. Grayson buys Maniac a zep. ___
7. Maniac asks for some butterscoth Krimpets. ___
8. Grayson finds Maniac. ___
9. Grayson lugs Maniac into the baseball equipment room. ___
10. Grayson gives Maniac some chicken noodle soup. ___

F) Fill in the numbered clues to help you find the larger word.

Example: What season has four letters? Write the first letter in space #3, the second letter in space #5, the third/fourth letter in space #6.

1	2	3	4	5	6	7
b	u	f	f	a	l	o

3,5,6,6 - a season; 1,5,6,6 a spherical body; 2,4,7 - an unidentified flying object

1	2	3	4	5	6	7	8	9	10	11	12

12,9,10 - very warm; 11,9,1 - an ear of corn; 8,6,2,7,3 - a hard thin coating; 4,5,7,4 - an exam or quiz

1	2	3	4	5	6	7	8	9	10

1,9,3,8,10 - coming to an end; 4,6,8,2,10 - any of the cereals;

by Jerry Spinelli

A) **Illustrate** and **name** what Maniac had for dinner. Also **show** what Grayson had.

B) **Draw** and **label** a short for one team Grayson played on.

Maniac Magee
by Jerry Spinelli

A) Improve these sentences by correcting the faulty parallelism.

1. Maniac would like camping, hiking and to go fishing. _____

_____

_____

2. Grayson lives at the Y, drives the park pickup and butterscotch Krimpets are his favorite. _____

_____

_____

3. They raised fences, mended fences hauled stone, patched asphalt and painted. _____

_____

_____

4. All Maniac wanted was food and a roof over his head. _____

_____

_____

B) What surprising information about the Beales did Maniac tell Grayson?

_____

_____

C) Why did Maniac want Grayson to talk about himself?

_____

_____

_____

D) Tell some practical jokes that you could play.

1. _____

_____

_____

2. _____

_____

3. _____

_____

4. _____

_____

_____

E) What practical joke was played on Grayson?

_____

_____

_____

F) Explain what happened when Grayson Got his big chance (the saddest story).

_____

_____

_____

_____

MANIAC MAGEE
by Jerry Spinelli

Chapters 26 and 27 - Title: _____ Page 27

A) Illustrate the cover of one of the books Grayson and Maniac got from the library.

B) Where would you put your fingers to throw a:

CURVE BALL

FORK BALL

KNUCKLEBALL

FASTBALL

C) Can you figure out what books maniac read?

1. XLLPYLLP - _____

2. NFHRX - _____

3. NZGS - _____

4. GIZEVO - _____

5. NBHGVIRVH - _____

6. HKVOOVIH - _____

7. YRLTIZKSRVH - _____

8. ZHGILMLNB - _____

HINT: Z = A   L = O   THINK REVERSE

D) Sketch the following triangles.

Equilateral   **Right Angle**

Isosceles   **Scalene**

MANIAC MAGEE

by Jerry Spinelli

A) What did Grayson and Maniac teach each other?

_____

_____

_____

_____

B) Describe a "stopball".

_____

_____

_____

D) What is a self-fulfilling prophecy? Give an example.

_____

_____

_____

_____

E) What letters gave Grayson the most trouble?

_____

_____

C) Missing Vowels: These words are missing vowels. Sometimes they are the same but sometimes they are different.

1. d _ _ r
2. classr _ _ m
3. fift _ _ n
4. thr _ _
5. s _ _ med
6. z _ _
7. aftern _ _ ns
8. b _ _ k
9. s _ _ n
10. s _ _ n
11. _ q _ _ pm _ nt
12. h _ pp _ n
13. b _ s _ b _ ll
14. l _ ng _ r
15. gr _ _ nd _ rs
16. _ nstr _ ct _ _ n
17. c _ rl _ d
18. pr _ f _ ss _ r
19. cl _ _ m _ d
20. _ nv _ lv _ d

F) Missing Consonants: These words are missing consonants.

1. cla _ _ es
2. mi _ _ ing
3. sa _ _ le
4. pre _ _ _ y
5. di _ _ erent
6. sto _ _ ed
7. sy _ _ able
8. po _ _ el
9. bo _ _
10. bu _ _ on
11. a _ ythi _ g
12. _ e _ _ _ er
13. no _ _ e _
14. _ rinci _ al
15. _ i _ teen
16. par _ - _ ime
17. _ a _ ar
18. _ ovl _ orth
19. _ lack _ oard
20. co _ so _ a _ t

MANIAC MAGEE
by Jerry Spinelli

A) Draw and **name** the things Grayson brought to Maniac's place.

B) Illustrate and **label** the Thanksgiving dinner Grayson and Maniac had.

MANIAC MAGEE
by Jerry Spinelli

A) List some things for which you could say "A-men".

1. _____

2. _____

3. _____

4. _____

5. _____

6. _____

7. _____

8. _____

9. _____

10. _____

B) Find an example of personification in Chapter 29.

_____

_____

_____

_____

C) How did Grayson see himself after the Mud Hen game?

_____

_____

D) Why did Grayson whisper, "A-men"?

_____

_____

_____

E) Why was the dinner they had particularly appropriate?

_____

_____

_____

_____

F) Why did Maniac put a number on the band shell?

_____

_____

_____

_____

MANIAC MAGEE

by Jerry Spinelli

Chapters 30 and 31 - Title: _____ Page 31

A) Wherever there were a few vacant square inches, something Christmassy appeared. **Draw** and **color** several things that did or could appear.

B) **Illustrate** with color the Christmas presents that were exchanged.

Maniac Magee
by Jerry Spinelli

Chapters 30 and 31

A) Why was the tree in the woods decorated?

_____
_____
_____

B) Describe how the tree in the woods was decorated.

_____
_____
_____
_____
_____
_____

C) Name **ten** animals they visited on Christmas morning.

_____
_____
_____
_____
_____

D) What happened to Grayson?

_____
_____

How old was he? ____ years? ___ days?

_____
_____

E) Rearrange the two letter word groups to find

a) flowers
1. se, ro _____
2. ap, ag, dr, sn, on _____
3. we, lo, nf, su, rs _____
4. as, ni, tu, pe _____

b) dogs
1. ow, ch _____
2. he, sh, ep, rd _____
3. an, rm, be, do _____
4. ag, be, le _____

c) baseball
1. nt, bu_____
2. tt, ba, er _____
3. ng, le, si _____
4. ub, do, le _____
5. rs, de, el, fi in _____
6. ld, ie, tf, ou, er _____

F) There are over 30 baseball terms in this puzzle. Words go left to right and top to bottom. They do not go backwards.

```
        U G L O V E T
      R T R I P L E F O M
      Z B A T B I E F O U L T
    D U G O U T A C D T M A F
    R U N E N L C D B B F A N S L
    H I T O F L H O A S I G N S K
    Q M S P G P E F T A E S R T D
    C A T C H E R F T S L I D E R
    R S R U I N F I E L D N P A I
    T K I R H O M E R U N G L L L
    L U K V S W H B Y I X L A J L
    V E E C F O O U B L E T G
      M P I C K O F F D H K E
      N C H A N G E U P I
        O T H R O W E J
```

MANIAC MAGEE

by Jerry Spinelli

Chapter 32 - Title: _____ Page 33

A) What happened to Grayson?

C) What was Grayson's favorite book?

B) Who was at the funeral?

D) What did Maniac do?

E) There are at least 30 words in this puzzle. Words read left to right. Individual rows may slide up or down to indicate new letter(s) in the middle. Words may be 3,4,5 or 6 letters long.

B	R	A	O	R	G
C	E	E	K	N	D
S	H	I	M	I	S
T	P	O	P	E	T
F	L	L	R	S	M

1. _____   9. _____   17. _____
2. _____   10. _____   18. _____
3. _____   11. _____   19. _____
4. _____   12. _____   20. _____
5. _____   13. _____   21. _____
6. _____   14. _____   22. _____
7. _____   15. _____   23. _____
8. _____   16. _____   24. _____

MANIAC MAGEE

by Jerry Spinelli

A) **Sketch** a map showing places were Maniac had wandered. Include a legend, compass rose, a scale. **Name** roads and highways that connect these places.

MANIAC MAGEE
by Jerry Spinelli

Chapters 33 and 34 Page 35

A) Match the prefixes with the correct root word.

re; re; in; un; un; mis; mis; be; be; trans; in; dis; dis; non; non; ex; ex; pre; pre; trans

1. ___grace
2. ___correct
3. ___claim
4. ___label
5. ___gain
6. ___gin
7. ___port
8. ___toxic
9. ___fold
10. ___active

11. ___view
12. ___like
13. ___fiction
14. ___cept
15. ___read
16. ___devil
17. ___fusion
18. ___lucky
19. ___rinse
20. ___cede

B) How would you describe Maniac's state of mind in January?

_____

_____

_____

C) Where did Maniac settle?

_____

_____

_____

D) Punctuate the following:

1. where is it demanded russell glancing around

2. were feeling for a gun russell explained

3. where have you been he yelled

4. we stold it screecher blurted

5. get a load of this meatball said the one with a front tooth missing he walks around with a blanket on hey meatball whyn't bring your mattress

E) Whose voices did Maniac hear during the second night?

_____

_____

_____

_____

_____

F) Explain the relationship between big John and the runaways.

_____

_____

_____

_____

MANIAC MAGEE

by Jerry Spinelli

A) Design your own hamburger. Give it a special **name**. **Label** the ingredients.

B) Draw what was behind Finsterwald's door.

MANIAC MAGEE

by Jerry Spinelli

Chapters 35 and 36

A) Why did Maniac tell the story of the stopball?

_____
_____
_____
_____

B) Describe in 25 words or less the McNab home.

_____
_____
_____
_____
_____

C) Make words from letters in the circle. The letters "**ie**" must be in every word.

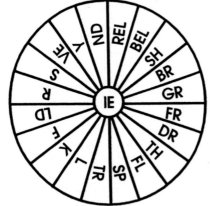

1. _____   7. _____   13. _____
2. _____   8. _____   14. _____
3. _____   9. _____   15. _____
4. _____   10. _____   16. _____
5. _____   11. _____   17. _____
6. _____   12. _____   18. _____

D) Each page shows words from a dictionary. Cross out the words that do not fit.

fraud	gable
fraud	fun
freeze	funeral
four	gaberdine
friend	gain
frolic	game
fulfill	gable

lip	lone
lip	long
list	lock
lion	locust
list	lop
live	luck
lizar	lone

E) Tell how Maniac got Russell and Piper to stay in school.

_____
_____
_____
_____
_____

F) Describe a scary experience that you have had.

_____
_____
_____
_____
_____

MANIAC MAGEE
by Jerry Spinelli

A) Illustrate one of Maniac's historic feats.

B) Draw the scene at the end of the race.

MANIAC MAGEE
by Jerry Spinelli

Chapters 33 and 34

A) What was the most perilous challenge of all?

_____

_____

B) Show what day it was.

_____

_____

C) Write down some other sayings instead of honky donkey. (Make sure they rhyme.) Nonsense ones will work.

1. _____ _____

2. _____ _____

3. _____ _____

4. _____ _____

5. _____ _____

6. _____ _____

7. _____ _____

8. _____ _____

9. _____ _____

10. _____ _____

D) How did Mars Bars hope to humiliate Maniac?

_____

_____

E) Comment on Maniac's decision of how to win the race.

_____

_____

_____

_____

F) Write sentences to show correct usage.

1. A   An   And

_____

_____

2. Buy   By

_____

_____

3. Know   No

_____

_____

4. New   Knew

_____

_____

5. It's   Its

_____

_____

MANIAC MAGEE
by Jerry Spinelli

Chapters 39 and 40 - Title: _____   Page 40

A) Illustrate the scene when Russell and Piper met Maniac after he crossed Hector Street. Write what they said to him.

B) Sketch what you would be facing after you busted through the steel door.

MANIAC MAGEE
by Jerry Spinelli

Chapters 39 and 40

A) Write the meanings of the following words.

ludicrous - _____

_____

goaded - _____

_____

shenanigans - _____

_____

frenzied - _____

_____

prodded - _____

_____

protruding - _____

_____

D) Can you find a rhyming pair of words for:

1. an unhappy father _____

2. a fat fish _____

3. a counterfeit horse _____

4. a boisterous kid _____

5. a joyful father _____

6. a confused amphibian _____

7. chubby beagle _____

8. a royal hound _____

9. irritable employer _____

10. an unreal sausage _____

B) Explain the opening sentence of Chapter 39.

_____

_____

_____

E) Why did Maniac lose his cool with the McNab boys?

_____

_____

_____

C) What was the something else in the house that smelled worse than the garbage?

_____

_____

F) Whom will Maniac bring to the party?

_____

_____

_____

MANIAC MAGEE

by Jerry Spinelli

Chapters 41 and 42 - Title: _____   Page 42

A) **Illustrate** the dinner at the Pickwells. Name everyone.

B) What does Mars Bar's "evil eye" make come to a complete stop. **Illustrate** your answer.

C) **Draw** Piper's birthday present.

MANIAC MAGEE
by Jerry Spinelli

A) What are some things you could tell Mars Bar to prove that he ain't so bad?

B) How was Mars Bar received in the Pickwell home?

_____

_____

C) How will Mars Bar be received in Fort McNab?

_____

_____

_____

D) Create your own similes.

1. as bad as _____

2. as tough as _____

3. as scared as _____

4. as white as _____

5. as black as _____

6. as evil as _____

7. as cruel as _____

8. as nervous as _____

9. as mad as _____

10. as smooth as _____

E) Describe what happened at Piper's party.

_____

_____

_____

_____

_____

_____

F) Why is Mars Bar more than bad - he's good?

_____

_____

_____

_____

_____

MANIAC MAGEE
by Jerry Spinelli

A) Sketch some backyards that Maniac knew.

B) Illustrate Russell's predicament.

MANIAC MAGEE
by Jerry Spinelli

A) Name **six** places Maniac slept.

1. _____   4. _____

2. _____   5. _____

3. _____   6. _____

B) What does your backyard say about you?

_____

_____

_____

C) Make a **two** to **seven** words using letters in each row. **Bonus** of 50 points if seven letters. Add the values and put total on the right.

Total

P_3	C_2	E_1	E_1	A_1	S_1	D_2

O_1	I_1	G_2	N_1	H_4	T_1	N_1

R_1	R_1	E_1	E_1	E_1	S_1	V_5

L_1	L_1	S_1	R_1	M_3	A_1	E_1

D) Tell how Maniac and Mars Bar used to meet each other.

1. _____
   _____

2. _____
   _____

3. _____
   _____

4. _____
   _____

5. _____

E) Describe Maniac's rescue of Russell.

_____

_____

F) Write the **plural** form.

1. bench _____
2. themself _____
3. porch _____
4. family _____
5. canyon _____
6. alleyway _____
7. gondola _____
8. friend _____
9. lady _____
10. baby _____
11. potato _____
12. tomato _____

Maniac Magee
by Jerry Spinelli

A) Fill in the blank spaces. Words begin with letters in the stated categories.

Category	A	O	M	R	S	T
Food						
Animals						
Games						
Foreign Places						
?						

B) Draw and name **five** animals that are in the zoo.

Maniac Magee

by Jerry Spinelli

A) Who visited Maniac? Tell why he did it.

_____

_____

_____

_____

B) Who changed Maniac's decision? Tell how it was done.

_____

_____

_____

C) State Mars Bars new name and the reason for changing it.

_____

_____

_____

D) What happened to Maniac McGee?

_____

_____

_____

_____

E) Be Creative. Fill in the word boxes below.

H I L L

J O S H

F) Write the **homonyms** for the words below.

1. air - _____
2. birth - _____
3. cache - _____
4. clue - _____
5. ate - _____
6. forth - _____
7. gneiss - _____
8. isle - _____
9. knight - _____
10. rap - _____
11. tense - _____

Maniac Magee

by Jerry Spinelli

Answer Key

Just The Facts: *(page 9)*
1. Maniac Magee
2. Jerry Spinelli
3. John Newbery Medal
4. a) Dump Days
   b) Jason and Marceline
   c) Night of the Whale
   d) Space Station Seventh Grade
   e) Who Put That Hair in My Toothbrush?
5. Little, Brown and Company
6. United States, Canada, England
7. Ray and Jerry Lincoln
8. Maniac Magee
9. East Side - West Side
10. 0-316-80722-2

Chapter 1 & 2 - Meet Maniac: *(page 10)*
A) a house in Bridgeport
B) killed when a trolley car plunged into Schuylkill River
C) Talk! Talk, will ya! Talk! Talk! Talk!
D) 200 miles
E) 10 000
F) Maniac jogging and saying, "Hi"

Chapter 1 & 2: *(page 11)*
A) Jeffrey Lionel Magee
B) With his Aunt Dot and Uncle Dan in Holidaysburg, Pennsylvania
C) He couldn't stand them not talking to each other and not caring about each other.
D) In Two Mills
E) Answers may vary.
F) 1. Little Jeffrey was shipped off to his nearest relatives Aunt Dot and Uncle Dan.
   2. As he passed them he said, "Hi".
   3. They lived in Holidaysburg in the western part of Pennsylvania.
   4. Two mills is right across the Schuylkill River from Bridgeport.
   5. The song they sang was "Talk to the Animals".

Chapters 3 & 4 - Jeffrey's Appearances: *(page 12)*
A) Books fiction and non fiction - who-did-it, let's-be-friends, what-is-it, how-not-to-books, regular kids books, a volume of A encyclopedia
B) About a dozen players on the field - probably coach on the sideline, quarterback Brian Denehy, 60 yards downfield James "Hands" Down (on the sideline) Jeffrey runs the other way for a touchdown. Students could name other people e.g. Ricky the Monster Man

Chapters 3&4: *(page 13)*
A) The East End was black; the West End was white.
B) Whites don't go to the East End.
C) Answers may vary.
D) Answers may vary.
E) Except for the punt he had done everything with one hand, the other hand was holding a book.
F)
1. friendly	2. reducing	3. slammed
4. hesitated	5. truly	6. stared
7. taking	8. carried	9. ripped
10. weaving	11. stunned	12. argument
13. dropping	14. begging	15. fatter

Chapter 5 & 6 - Two Places the Kid Visits: *(page 14)*
A) tennis balls, baseballs, footballs, Frisbees, model airplanes and one-way boomerangs
B) Mr. & Mrs. Pickwell, Grandmother & Grandfather Pickwell, Great-grandfather Pickwell, a taxi driver, Jeffrey, Didi, Dominic, Duke, Donald, Dion, Deirdre & four more Pickwell children whose names probably start with "D" (17)
C) He was running not on the wooden ties or the cinders but on the steel rails.

Chapters 5 & 6: *(page 15)*
A) A violent trembling of the body especially in the extremities - by going into Finsterwald's yard.
B) He was hoisted over the backyard fence of Finsterwalds and got the "finsterwallies".
C) This is an exercise in commas:
   1. the back door, the windows, and the dark green shades.
   2. the dump, the creek, the tracks, and from Red Hill;
   3. Answers may vary.
   4. Answers may vary.
   5. Answers may vary.
D)
| 1. G | 2. D | 3. F | 4. H |
| 5. B | 6. E | 7. C | 8. A |
E) It wasn't loud or screechy - it was a simple two - note job - one high and one low
F) He hoisted Arnold's body over his shoulder and hauled him out of the backyard and put him in the front yard.

Chapters 7 & 8 - Why Maniac: *(page 16)*
A) The positions are catcher, pitcher, first base, second base, shortstop, third base, left field, center field, right field. First - landed in second base; rolled to center field; second - deep left center, bounced over the fence; third - cleared the fence (no designation); fourth, fifth, sixth -

home runs; seventh center field; eighth - bunt in front of plate - third base side.

B) Name of Province (State), Country, Title of Certificate, Person's Name, Date of Birth, Birthplace, Date of Registration, Date of Issue, Sex, Certificate Number, Registration Number, Name of Registrar, Provincial Seal, Form Number

* This should be discussed prior to the assignment. On the back of the certificate is a drawing of a province or state.

Chapters 7 & 8: *(page 17)*

A)
1.	a fastball	1.	(A.C.)
2.	runt	2.	(A.C.)
3.	wandering	3.	(A.C.)
4.	frog (A.C.)	4.	(A.C.)

B) Answers may vary - conceited, a braggart

C) Answers may vary - happy

D) Probably because his activity was excessive

E) Children in France and Germany decided to conquer the Holy Land in 1212. Many died or were sold into slavery. Over 50 000 children were involved.

F) Answers may vary - some answers w-hen, w-as, w-on, t-here, t-hem, s-truck, s-aid, s-till

Chapters 9 & 10 - Two Gangs: *(page 18)*

Students choose any six in this order:

A) the dump; mountain range of stone piles; into the trees; skiing down a steep bank; into the creek; through the trees and picker bushes; past armory jeeps; out to park boulevard; past an Italian restaurant; bakery; row houses; streets; alleys; cars; porches; windows; blurred faces

B) Assume the Thompson boy was eating a Mars Bars, others are student responses.

Chapters 9 & 10: *(page 19)*

A) He couldn't stand having this blemish on his record. - If you beat a kid up, it's the same as striking him out.

B) They knew Maniac wouldn't cross into the East End and if he did he would get beat up.

C) Mars Bar Thompson

D) An East End lady intervened.

E) No one would chomp on Mars's bar. White kids would not put their mouths where black kids had theirs - be it soda bottles, spoons or candy bars. Besides Maniac had chomped right over Mars Bar's own bite marks.

F) Answers may vary.

G) Answers are found in the book e.g. 1. He was down by Red Hill and heading away from them, book in hand. 2. He wobbled once, leaped from the rail to the ground and took off. 3. People did cross the line now and then, especially if

they were adults and it was daylight. 4. The kid hadn't even gone for the unused end but had chomped right over Mars Bar's own bite marks.

Chapters 11 & 12 - The Beales: *(page 20)*

A) Answers may vary - perhaps a dedication page or a puzzle page or the last page. Instead of filling in their favorite pages - perhaps idea on Amanda's favorite pages.

B) Hester was standing on the countertop, Lester was standing below her on a chair. A shattered glass jar and some stringy pale-colored glop was on the floor.

Chapters 11 & 12: *(page 21)*

A) Amanda showed up, accused Mars Bar of ripping her book, kicked him in the sneakers and caused him to leave.

B) as a broken wing of a bird or a pet out in the rain

C) Answers may vary

D)
1.	it's	8.	wasn't
2.	they're	9.	didn't
3.	who's	10.	that's
4.	you're	11.	what's
5.	couldn't	12.	I'm
6.	we'll	13.	there's
7.	weren't	14.	don't

E) He claimed that he lived in a house and Mr. Beale knew that wasn't true.

F) He made a U-turn and took Maniac to his home.

Chapters 13 & 14 - A Happy Time: *(page 22)*

A) Could be a great small group assignment to be completed on large sheets of white paper. Look for different pizza combinations.

B) Answers may vary - Makes a great art lesson.

Chapters 13 & 14: *(page 23)*

A) Answers may vary - The not so true homonym is petal.

B) played with the little ones, read the stories, taught them things, took dog out for a walk, did the dishes, carried out the trash, mowed the grass, cleaned up his spills, turned out lights, put toothpaste cap back or flushed the toilet and kept his room clean

C) Answers may vary.

D) new sneakers, quietness of his footsteps, early morning silence and solitude, later day noise, hissing pancake batter, the noise of the church, Fourth of July block party, the colors of East End. The warm brown of Mrs. Beale's thumb under creamy white icing, playing the summer days away.

E) gingersnap, light fudge, acorn, butter rum, cinnamon, and burnt orange

F)
1. unicorn
2. bicycle
3. trio
4. quartet
5. pentathlon
6. hexagon
7. September
8. octopus
9. November
10. decimal
11. century

Chapters 15 & 16 - Blind: *(page 24)*

A) Do it, man! Smoke them suckas! Poke 'em! Joke 'em! You bad - dudin' it, You the baddest! Five me, jude! and two student responses.

B) In order to do this lesson, attention should be paid to: cleanliness of hands, utensils and work area. Discussion on the oven temperature, list of the ingredients and the quantity of each, directions on how to mix ingredients and the cooking directions.

Chapters 15 & 16: *(page 25)*

A) He lived with the Beales in a black neighborhood; Ran the streets before the fathers went out; He could pole ax a stickball like a twelfth grader; Catch a football like "Hands" Down; Was allergic to pizza; Jumped up in Church and shouts, "Hallelujah! Amen!"; Could untie knots quickly; Run like a squirrel; Could juke, jive, spin, dance, and dart.

B) Answers may vary.

C) Answers may vary.

D)
1. take charge of the situation
2. unrealistic expectations
3. short change someone to pay someone else
4. be mistaken
5. so busy in what you're doing to see other things

E) Answers may vary, i.e. - a healthy attitude

F) big kids being showed up by little kids, big kids laughing at big kids being shown up by little kids, kids who are allergic to pizza, kids that are different, kids who do dishes, kids who never watch Saturday morning cartoons or kids of another color.

Chapters 17 & 18 - Please Stay: *(page 26)*

A) Fire hydrant - block party, swimming pool, radios, people - lemonade, Kool-Aid, bodies, skin, colors, water, gleaming, buttery, warm, cool, wet, screaming, happy, clothes

B) too, buttery, croaking, black-sheep - Cobble's Knot

C) Blackboard outline - Name of library - borrower's name, address, phone number, city seal, bar code, Library conditions i.e. Borrower responsible for materials

Chapters 17 & 18: *(page 27)*

A) He didn't want Maniac on the Black Zone. He says, "Never enough, is it, Whitey

B) ISHBELLY Go Home

C) It was only a nutty old coot. They did my mother a favor. You'll starve, you'll freeze, what abouta pillow - a bathroom.

D) Answers may vary.

E) I'm incubating an egg - Student response

F) Answers may vary, i.e. under the table, through the window - Responses are to be used in a later exercise.

Chapters 19 & 20 - The Challenge: *(page 28)*

A) The prize is one large pizza per week for a year.

B) Pizza, zeps, steak sandwiches, strombolis, soda are mentioned.

Chapters 19 & 20: *(page 29)*

A) green, arena, aroma, flock, false, flora, alien, heavy, skunk, - groceries

B) Mr. Cobble saw a knot dangling from the flagpole. He noticed what an unusual knot it was and offered a prize to anyone who could untangle it.

C) It was about the size of a lopsided volleyball. It was made of string and had many twists and turns. When Maniac saw it, it was grimy, mouldy and crusted over.

D) The touch of a surgeon, the alertness of an owl, the cunning of three foxes and the foresight of a grand master in chess.

E) Some said he viewed it as an old pal just playing a trick on him, others said he viewed it as a worthy opponent.

F) Answers may vary - Could they identify the word the phrase describes and name the type of phrase?

Chapter 21 - Out of Town: *(page 30)*

A) Hector Street runs north and south. Some streets in East End are East Chestnut, East Marshall, Green Street, Arch Street and Sycamore. In the West End- Oriole. He walked west on Sycamore In the WestEnd - Oriole. He walked west on Sycamore to Hector and north on Hector right in the middle of the street.

B) Africa, Alaska, Algebra, Algeria, Amazon, Anableps, Ankara, Anzio, Apple, Aristotle, Auk, Azores

C) Answers may vary.

Chapter 21: *(page 31)*

A)
1. thanks   2. started   3. across
4. stomach, normal, tables, genetic, scarlet, front, undone, never, budget, truthful, leopard, challenge, earned

B) (41/2 X 500) + (4 X 12.5)= 2250 + 50
   = 2300m
   = 2.3 km
   = 23 000 dm
   = 230 000 cm
   = 2 300 000 mm
C) The home made confetti was made from the pages of Amanda's Encyclopedia A.
D) Answers may vary.
E) Answers may vary.
F) He felt no one wanted him.

Chapters 22 & 23 - Meet Grayson: *(page 32)*
A) Maniac was found outside the buffalo compound. There is a mother and baby buffalo in the compound. There is a lean to in the compound. A chain link fence separates them.
B) Ten packs of three or 30.

Chapters 22 & 23: *(page 33)*
A) Grayson
B) He was homeless but he mistakenly climbed into the buffalo area rather than the deer area.
C) He thought that Maniac would stay with him.
D) In the daytime it was okay but at night it emptied out everyone went home; and he didn't want one without the other.
E) 6,10,2,4,1,8,9,3,5,7
F) fall, ball, ufo - buffalo
   hot, cob, crust, test - butterscotch
   final, grain, fen - fingernail

Chapters 24 & 25 - Play Ball: *(page 34)*
A) meatloaf and gravy, mashed potatoes, zucchini, salad and coconut custard pie - cup of coffee
B) Pedukah Twin Oaks, Natchez Pelicans, Jesup Georgia Browns, Raredo Lariats, Toledo Mud Hens (three innings) and Guanajuato (no name given)

Chapters 24 & 25: *(page 35)*
A) Suggested answers:
   1. Maniac would like camping, hiking and fishing.
   2. Grayson lives at the Y, drives the park pickup and loves butterscotch Krimpets.
   3. They raised fences, mended fences, hauled stone, patched asphalt, and painted posts.
   4. All Maniac wanted was food and shelter.
B) That they ate the same foods, had the same furniture as white people.
C) He wanted Grayson to feel good about himself (doesn't everyone when they talk about themselves)
D) Answers may vary.
E) He was told that he could eat the first meal free at the Blue Star restaurant. He had to do dishes to pay for the meal.

F) His curve ball wasn't curving, his sinker wasn't sinking, and his knuckle wasn't knuckling. He was in the showers before the third inning was over.

Chapters 26 & 27 - Teaching Each Other: *(page 36)*
A) They bought about twenty picture books. Some suggested ones - "The Story of Babar", "Mike Mulligan's Steam Shovel" - "The Little Engine that could".
B) **Curveball** - index and forefinger across seam, thumb behind other seam
   Forkball - index and forefinger on either side of seam
   Knuckleball - index, fore and middle fingertips on the seams
   Fastball - index and forefinger tips on the seams
C) To solve the code, write letters of the alphabet in reverse order to match natural order i.e. A = Z, B = Y, C = X,

   1. cookbook   5. mysteries
   2. music   6. spellers
   3. math   7. biographies
   4. travel   8. astronomy

D)

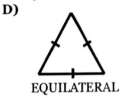

EQUILATERAL   RIGHT ANGLE

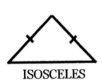

ISOSCELES   SCALENE

Chapters 26 & 27: *(page 37)*
A) Grayson taught Maniac how to spray liners to the opposite field; how to get a jump on a line on a long fly; how to throw a curveball. Maniac taught Grayson how to read.
B) The ball floats to the plate and when its over the plate it stops.
C)
   1. door   11. equipment
   2. classroom   12. happen
   3. fifteen   13. baseball
   4. three   14. longer
   5. seemed   15. grounders
   6. zoo   16. instruction
   7. afternoons   17. curled
   8. book   18. professor
   9. seen   19. claimed
   10. soon   20. involved

D) It's one that is said and the person makes it come true. The teacher said the kids would never be able to read so they quit trying and never did learn how to read.

E) the vowels

F)
1. classes
2. missing
3. saddle
4. pretty
5. different
6. stopped
7. syllable
8. pommel
9. boss
10. button
11. anything
12. pepper
13. nodded
14. principal
15. fifteen
16. part time
17. Babar
18. Woolworth
19. blackboard
20. consonant

Chapters 28 & 29 - Amen: *(page 38)*

A) toaster oven, a chest of drawers, a space heater, a two foot refrigerator, hundreds of paper dishes and plastic utensils, blankets, and a mat to sleep on

B) roast chicken, gravy, cranberry sauce, applesauce, Spaghetti O's, raisins, pumpkin pie, and butterscotch Krimpets

Chapters 28 & 29: *(page 39)*

A) Answers may vary.

B) Two Mills has an ear, chin, stomach, the arctic air laid panes of ice

C) a failure

D) He liked having Maniac with him and the fact that Maniac put a blanket over him.

E) It was Thanksgiving and they were thankful for what they had.

F) He wanted an address and he thought he had a home.

Chapters 30 & 31 - Gifts: *(page 40)*

A) a match box criche, a porcelain Santa, a partridge in a pear tree appeared, answers may vary.

B) Maniac gave Grayson a pair of gloves, a woolen cap, a blue covered book with stick figures on it and the title "The Man Who Struck Out Willie Mays". Grayson gave Maniac a pair of gloves, a box of butterscotch Krimpets, a brand new baseball, and his baseball glove.

Chapters 30 & 31: *(page 41)*

A) The room was too small to hold their Christmas spirit.

B) red and yellow necklaces of bittersweet pinecones, wine red sumac berries, bird bodied boats of milkweed and thumb sized goblets of Queen Anne's Lace

C) muskrats, ducks, buffalo, and other zoo animals (not named)

D) Grayson died five days after Christmas December 30. He was 64 years old
64 X 365 = 3 360 + 15 - 23 375 days

E)
a) flowers	b) dogs	c) baseball
1. rose	1. chow	1. bunt
2. snapdragon	2. shepherd	2. batter
3. sunflowers	3. doberman	3. single
4. petunias	4. beagle	4. double
		5. infielders
		6. outfielder

F) Answers may vary - 34 possible answers here - pitcher, catcher, dugout, bunt, bullpen, bat, tag, run, hit, infield, outfield, battery, curve, slider, signs, homerun, homer, drill, triple, single, double, fans, pick off, steal, strike, plate, mask, pitch, catch, foul, lead off, throw, change up, glove

Chapter 32 - Grayson: *(page)42*

A) Grayson died.

B) six pallbearers, Maniac, man from the funeral home, two men off to the side

C) Mike Mulligan's Steam Shovel

D) He ran away

E) Answers may vary - 30 suggested answers, 24 required: broke, floor, hopes, spoke, spore, pope, him, shore, loon, shop, shores, ham, chop, shapes, hike, flop, shape, hip, slop, seem, hire, shape, beam, rare, ship, apes, poke, pop, hope, trap

Chapters 33 & 34 - An Old Friend: *(page 43)*

Places in the chapter: Bridgeport, Conshohocken, East Norriton, West Norriton, Jeffersonville, Plymouth, Worcester, Bridgeport is across the Schuylkill River from Two Mills. Valley Forge was five or six miles for Two Mills. Stoney Creek is also mentioned.

Chapters 33 & 34: *(page 44)*

A) Suggested answers:
1. disgrace
2. incorrect
3. exclaim
4. mislabel
5. regain
6. begin
7. transport
8. nontoxic
9. unfold
10. inactive
11. review
12. dislike
13. nonfiction
14. except
15. misread
16. bedevil
17. transfusion
18. unlucky
19. prerinse
20. precede

B) He was despondent and ready to die.

C) in a log and mortar cabin in Valley Forge

D)
1. "Where is it?" demanded Russell, glancing around.
2. "We're feelin' for a gun?", Russell explained.
3. "Where you been?" he yelled.
4. "We stold it!" Screecher blurted.

5. "Get a load of this meatball," said the one with a front tooth missing." He walks around with a blanket on. Hey meatball, why'nt you bring your mattress?"
E) Screecher and Missing Tooth (two little boys)
F) They were brothers. Big John was the pitcher in Two Mills.

Chapters 35 & 36 - The McNabs: *(page 45)*
A) Answers may vary.
B) Answers may vary.

Chapters 35 & 36: *(page 46)*
A) He wanted to remain friends with John; he wanted Russell and Piper to admire their brother; he wanted John to maintain his self respect.
B) The house was a pig sty. It smelled and there was garbage all over. Roaches were everywhere.
C) Answers may vary - 24 suggested answers: relief, thief, belief, friend, fries, flies, tries, spies, dries, thieves, believes, brief, briefs, grief, grieve, grieves, field, shield, fields, shields, believer, lies, skies, belies, relies
D) four, gain, game, lion, long, lop, luck
E) Pizza for a week, a week to stay in Finsterwald's backyard for ten minutes, two weeks for knocking on the front door.
F) Answers may vary.

Chapters 37 & 38 - The Race: *(page 47)*
A) Historic feats could be: at twenty paces hit a telephone pole with a stone 61 times in a row; beat a freight train in a race; walk barefoot through a rat infested dump; stick your arm in a mysterious hole for 60 seconds; climb into the bison pen and kiss the baby or a made up one.
B) Maniac won the race but at the end he was backwards facing Mars Bars

Chapters 37 & 38: *(page 48)*
A) To go into the East End
B) It was the day of the worms.
C) Answers may vary - e.g. lorsey horsey or mookey lookey
D) By beating him in a race
E) **Stupid** - it humiliated Mars Bars or **dangerous** - as he was in the East End or **vengeful** - he felt better to humiliate him this way or answers may vary
F) Use "**a**" before a word beginning with a consonant; "**an**" before a word beginning with a vowel, "**and**" joins two words or ideas. "**Buy**" means to purchase something "**by**" means near or before

"**know**" - means to have understanding; "**knew**" - is past tense of "know" "**no**" is a negative,": "**new**" means recent "**it's**" means it is; "**its**" shows ownership

Chapters 39 & 40 - A Party Guest: *(page 49)*
A) R: "Maniac! You're alive!"
P: "We thought they got ya! We thought they slit your throat!"
R: "We thought they strangled ya and pulled yer tongue out!"
P: "We thought they chopped yer head off and...and..."
R: "And boiled ya!"
P: "Yeah, boiled ya!"
R: "And drunk yer blood!"
P: "Yeah!"
R: "And drunk yer brains!"
B) You would be facing a cinder block wall with some gunnery slots in it.

Chapters 39 & 40: *(page 50)*
A) **ludricrous** - funny, comical, goaded - to urge on **shenanigans** - fooling around, frenzied - frantic **prodded** - urged on, protruding - sticking out
B) The warm weather of April was cold as it was delayed two weeks.
C) prejudice
D)
1. a sad dad
2. stout trout
3. a phoney pony
4. a wild child
5. a happy pappy
6. a groggy froggy
7. a round hound
8. a regal beagle
9. a cross boss
10. a phoney baloney
E) He lost his cool when they used Grayson's glove for a football.
F) Answers may vary.

Chapter 41 & 42 - The Party: *(page 51)*
A) The people mentioned are Maniac, Mars Bars, a golf caddie, Mrs. Pickwell and Dolly. Answers may vary for the rest.
B) 23 cars, several bicycles, and a bus
C) a compass

Chapters 41 & 42: *(page 52)*
A) Answers may vary - e.g. some students might respond they could go to the dentist and Mars Bar couldn't.
B) He was invited to dinner and a fuss was made over him.
C) Answers may vary.
D) Answers may vary.
E) They played "Rebels" - whites in the pillbox, blacks outside. A cobra jumped from the hole in the ceiling and scared Maniac and Mars Bar. An argument ensued and Mars Bar and Maniac left the McNabs.

F) Mars Bar was trembling as he was scared, however he was putting on a brave front and seemingly struggling to fight the Cobras.

Chapters 43 & 44 - Running: *(page 53)*
A) Backyards had flowers, weeds, junk, pet houses, tree houses, vegetable gardens, rubber tires, shaggy grass, desert, sparse grass, trim grass

B) Russell was stranded in the trolley trestle that spanned the river.

Chapters 43 & 44: *(page 54)*
A) buffalo shed, bandshell benches, pavilion, backyards, back porches, or a kitchen

B) Answers may vary.

C) seven letter words are escaped, nothing, reserve, smaller

D) 1. running into each other
  2. running the same route a block apart
  3. down same street same time same direction but on opposite sides
  4. side by side
  5. dovetailed

E) He walked away.

F) benches, themselves, porches, families, canyons, alleyways, gondolas, friends, ladies, babies, potatoes, tomatoes

Chapters 45 & 46 - Home: *(page 55)*
A) Answers may vary - e.g. apple, orange, melon, raspberry, steak, taco

B) buffalo, crickets, fireflies, emu, prairie dogs, eagle

Chapters 45 & 46: *(page 56)*
A) Mars Bar to ask him why he didn't go after the kid and to ask him to come home with him.

B) **Amanda Beale** - She insisted he did not have a choice.

C) **Snickers** - how bad can you act if everybody's calling you that

D) He knew that finally at long last someone was calling him home.

E) Answers may vary.

F) 1. heir   5. eight   9. night
  2. berth   6. fourth   10. wrap
  3. cash   7. nice   11. tents
  4. do - dew   8. aisle - I'll

Publication Listing

Code # | **Title and Grade**

See Dealer or
www.onthemarkpress.com
For Pricing
1-800-463-6367

OTM-1492 Abel's Island NS 4-6
OTM-1131 Addition & Subtraction Drills Gr. 1-3
OTM-1128 Addition Drills Gr. 1-3
OTM-2504 Addition Gr. 1-3
OTM-14174 Adv. of Huckle Berry Finn NS 7-8
OTM-293 All About Dinosaurs Gr. 2
OTM-102 All About Mexico Gr. 4-6
OTM-120 All About the Ocean Gr. 5-7
OTM-249 All About the Sea Gr. 4-6
OTM-261 All About Weather Gr. 7-8
OTM-2110 All Kinds of Structures Gr. 1
OTM-601 Amazing Aztecs Gr. 4-6
OTM-1468 Amelia Bedelia NS 1-3
OTM-113 America The Beautiful Gr. 4-6
OTM-1457 Amish Adventure NS 7-8
OTM-602 Ancient China Gr. 4-6
OTM-618 Ancient Egypt Gr. 4-6
OTM-621 Ancient Greece Gr. 4-6
OTM-619 Ancient Rome Gr. 4-6
OTM-1453 Anne of Green Gables NS 7-8
OTM-14162 Arnold Lobel Author Study Gr. 2-3
OTM-1622 Australia B/W Pictures
OTM-105 Australia Gr. 5-8
OTM-14224 Banner in the Sky NS 7-8
OTM-401 Be Safe Not Sorry Gr. P-1
OTM-1409 Bear Tales Gr. 2-4
OTM-14202 Bears in Literature Gr. 1-3
OTM-1440 Beatrix Potter Gr. 2-4
OTM-14129 Beatrix Potter: Activity Biography Gr. 2-4
OTM-14257 Because of Winn-Dixie NS Gr. 4-6
OTM-14114 Best Christmas Pageant Ever NS Gr. 4-6
OTM-14107 Borrowers NS Gr. 4-6
OTM-1463 Bridge to Terabithia NS Gr. 4-6
OTM-2524 BTS Numeración Gr. 1-3
OTM-2525 BTS Adición Gr. 1-3
OTM-2526 BTS Sustracción Gr. 1-3
OTM-2527 BTS Fonética Gr. 1-3
OTM-2528 BTS Leer para Entender Gr. 1-3
OTM-2529 BTS Uso de las Mayúsculas y Reglas de Puntuación Gr. 1-3
OTM-2530 BTS Composición de Oraciones Gr. 1-3
OTM-2531 BTS Composici13n de Historias Gr. 1-3
OTM-14256 Bud, Not Buddy NS Gr. 4-6
OTM-1807 Building Word Families L.V. 1-2
OTM-1805 Building Word Families S.V. 1-2
OTM-14164 Call It Courage NS Gr. 7-8
OTM-1467 Call of the Wild NS Gr. 7-8
OTM-2507 Capitalization & Punctuation Gr. 1-3
OTM-14198 Captain Courageous NS Gr. 7-8
OTM-14154 Castle in the Attic NS Gr. 4-6
OTM-631 Castles & Kings Gr. 4-6
OTM-1434 Cats in Literature Gr. 3-6
OTM-14212 Cay NS Gr. 7-8
OTM-2107 Cells, Tissues & Organs Gr. 7-8
OTM-2101 Characteristics of Flight Gr. 4-6
OTM-1466 Charlie and Chocolate Factory NS Gr. 4-6
OTM-1423 Charlotte's Web NS Gr. 4-6
OTM-109 China Today Gr. 5-8
OTM-1470 Chocolate Fever NS Gr. 4-6
OTM-14241 Chocolate Touch NS Gr. 4-6
OTM-14104 Classical Poetry Gr. 7-12
OTM-811 Community Helpers Gr. 1-3
OTM-14183 Copper Sunrise NS Gr. 7-8
OTM-1486 Corduroy and Pocket Corduroy NS Gr. 1-3
OTM-234 Creatures of the Sea Gr. 2-4
OTM-14208 Curse of the Viking Grave NS 7-8
OTM-1121 Data Management Gr. 4-6
OTM-253 Dealing with Dinosaurs Gr. 4-6
OTM-14105 Dicken's Christmas NS Gr. 7-8
OTM-1621 Dinosaurs B/W Pictures
OTM-216 Dinosaurs Gr. 1
OTM-14175 Dinosaurs in Literature Gr. 1-3
OTM-2106 Diversity of Living Things Gr. 4-6
OTM-1127 Division Drills Gr. 4-6

OTM-287 Down by the Sea Gr. 1-3
OTM-1416 Dragons in Literature Gr. 3-6
OTM-2109 Earth's Crust Gr. 6-8
OTM-1612 Egypt B/W Pictures
OTM-14255 Egypt Game NS Gr. 4-6
OTM-628 Egyptians Today and Yesterday Gr. 2-3
OTM-2108 Electricity Gr. 4-6
OTM-285 Energy Gr. 4-6
OTM-2123 Environment Gr. 4-6
OTM-1812 ESL Teaching Ideas Gr. K-8
OTM-14258 Esperanza Rising NS Gr. 4-6
OTM-1822 Exercises in Grammar Gr. 6
OTM-1823 Exercises in Grammar Gr. 7
OTM-1824 Exercises in Grammar Gr. 8
OTM-620 Exploration Gr. 4-6
OTM-1054 Exploring Canada Gr. 1-3
OTM-1056 Exploring Canada Gr. 1-6
OTM-1055 Exploring Canada Gr. 4-6
OTM-820 Exploring My School and Community Gr. 1
OTM-1639 Fables B/W Pictures
OTM-1415 Fables Gr. 4-6
OTM-14168 First 100 Sight Words Gr. 1
OTM-14170 Flowers for Algernon NS Gr. 7-8
OTM-14128 Fly Away Home NS Gr. 4-6
OTM-405 Food: Fact, Fun & Fiction Gr. 1-3
OTM-406 Food: Nutrition & Invention Gr. 4-6
OTM-2118 Force and Motion Gr. 1-3
OTM-2119 Force and Motion Gr. 4-6
OTM-14172 Freckle Juice NS Gr. 1-3
OTM-14209 Giver, The NS Gr. 7-8
OTM-1114 Graph for all Seasons Gr. 1-3
OTM-1490 Great Expectations NS Gr. 7-8
OTM-14169 Great Gilly Hopkins NS Gr. 4-6
OTM-14238 Greek Mythology Gr. 7-8
OTM-2113 Growth & Change in Animals Gr. 2-3
OTM-2114 Growth & Change in Plants Gr. 2-3
OTM-14205 Harper Moon NS Gr. 7-8
OTM-14136 Hatchet NS Gr. 7-8
OTM-14184 Hobbit NS Gr. 7-8
OTM-14250 Holes NS Gr. 4-6
OTM-1848 How To Give a Presentation Gr. 4-6
OTM-14125 How To Teach Writing Through 7-9
OTM-1810 How To Write a Composition 6-10
OTM-1809 How To Write a Paragraph 5-10
OTM-1808 How To Write an Essay Gr. 7-12
OTM-1803 How To Write Poetry & Stories 4-6
OTM-407 Human Body Gr. 2-4
OTM-402 Human Body Gr. 4-6
OTM-605 In Days of Yore Gr. 4-6
OTM-606 In Pioneer Days Gr. 2-4
OTM-241 Incredible Dinosaurs Gr. P-1
OTM-14177 Incredible Journey NS Gr. 4-6
OTM-14100 Indian in the Cupboard NS Gr. 4-6
OTM-14193 Island of the Blue Dolphins NS 4-6
OTM-1465 James & The Giant Peach NS 4-6
OTM-1625 Japan B/W Pictures
OTM-106 Japan Gr. 5-8
OTM-1461 Julie of the Wolves NS Gr. 7-8
OTM-14140 Kids at Bailey School Gr. 2-4
OTM-298 Learning About Dinosaurs Gr. 3
OTM-1122 Learning About Measurement Gr. 1-3
OTM-1119 Learning About Money USA Gr. 1-3
OTM-1123 Learning About Numbers Gr. 1-3
OTM-269 Learning About Rocks and Soils Gr. 2-3
OTM-1108 Learning About Shapes Gr. 1-3
OTM-2100 Learning About Simple Machines Gr. 1-3
OTM-1104 Learning About the Calendar Gr. 2-3
OTM-1110 Learning About Time Gr. 1-3
OTM-1450 Legends Gr. 4-6
OTM-14130 Life & Adv. of Santa Claus NS 7-8
OTM-210 Life in a Pond Gr. 3-4
OTM-630 Life in the Middle Ages Gr. 7-8
OTM-2103 Light & Sound Gr. 4-6
OTM-14219 Light in the Forest NS Gr. 7-8
OTM-1446 Lion, Witch & the Wardrobe NS 4-6
OTM-1851 Literature Response Forms Gr. 1-3
OTM-1852 Literature Response Forms Gr. 4-6
OTM-14233 Little House on the Prairie NS 4-6
OTM-14109 Lost in the Barrens NS Gr. 7-8
OTM-14167 Magic School Bus Gr. 1-3
OTM-14247 Magic Treehouse Gr. 1-3
OTM-278 Magnets Gr. 3-5
OTM-403 Making Sense of Our Senses K-1
OTM-294 Mammals Gr. 1
OTM-295 Mammals Gr. 2
OTM-296 Mammals Gr. 3

OTM-297 Mammals Gr. 5-6
OTM-14160 Maniac Magee NS Gr. 4-6
OTM-119 Mapping Activities & Outlines! 4-8
OTM-117 Mapping Skills Gr. 1-3
OTM-107 Mapping Skills Gr. 4-6
OTM-2116 Matter & Materials Gr. 1-3
OTM-2117 Matter & Materials Gr. 4-6
OTM-1609 Medieval Life B/W Pictures
OTM-1413 Mice in Literature Gr. 3-5
OTM-14180 Midnight Fox NS Gr. 4-6
OTM-1118 Money Talks – Gr. 3-6
OTM-1497 Mouse & the Motorcycle NS 4-6
OTM-1494 Mr. Poppers Penguins NS Gr. 4-6
OTM-14201 Mrs. Frisby & Rats NS Gr. 4-6
OTM-1826 Multi-Level Spelling USA Gr. 3-6
OTM-1132 Multiplication & Division Drills 4-6
OTM-1130 Multiplication Drills Gr. 4-6
OTM-114 My Country! The USA! Gr. 2-4
OTM-1437 Mystery at Blackrock Island NS 7-8
OTM-14157 Nate the Great and Sticky Case NS Gr. 1-3
OTM-110 New Zealand Gr. 4-8
OTM-1475 Novel Ideas Gr. 4-6
OTM-14244 Number the Stars NS Gr. 4-6
OTM-2503 Numeration Gr. 1-3
OTM-14220 One in Middle Green Kangaroo NS Gr. 1-3
OTM-272 Our Trash Gr. 2-3
OTM-2121 Our Universe Gr. 5-8
OTM-286 Outer Space Gr. 1-2
OTM-118 Outline Maps of the World Gr. 1-8
OTM-1431 Owls in the Family NS Gr. 4-6
OTM-1452 Paperbag Princess NS Gr. 1-3
OTM-212 Passport to Australia Gr. 4-5
OTM-1804 Personal Spelling Dictionary Gr. 2-5
OTM-14171 Phoebe Gilman Author Study Gr. 2-3
OTM-2506 Phonics Gr. 1-3
OTM-1448 Pigs in Literature Gr. 2-4
OTM-1499 Pinballs NS Gr. 4-6
OTM-634 Pirates Gr. 4-6
OTM-2120 Planets Gr. 3-6
OTM-264 Prehistoric Times Gr. 4-6
OTM-1120 Probability & Inheritance Gr. 7-10
OTM-1426 Rabbits in Literature Gr. 2-4
OTM-1444 Ramona Quimby Age 8 NS 4-6
OTM-2508 Reading for Meaning Gr. 1-3
OTM-14234 Reading with Arthur Gr. 1-3
OTM-14200 Reading with Curious George 2-4
OTM-14230 Reading with Eric Carle Gr. 1-3
OTM-14251 Reading with Kenneth Oppel 4-6
OTM-1427 Reading with Mercer Mayer 1-2
OTM-14142 Reading with Robert Munsch 1-3
OTM-14225 River NS Gr. 7-8
OTM-265 Rocks & Minerals Gr. 4-6
OTM-14103 Sadako and 1 000 Paper Cranes NS Gr. 4-6
OTM-404 Safety Gr. 2-4
OTM-1442 Sarah Plain & Tall NS Gr. 4-6
OTM-1601 Sea Creatures B/W Pictures
OTM-279 Sea Creatures Gr. 1-3
OTM-1464 Secret Garden NS Gr. 4-6
OTM-2502 Sentence Writing Gr. 1-3
OTM-1430 Serendipity Series Gr. 3-5
OTM-1866 Shakespeare Shorts – Performing Arts Gr. 2-4
OTM-1867 Shakespeare Shorts – Performing Arts Gr. 4-6
OTM-1868 Shakespeare Shorts – Language Arts Gr. 2-4
OTM-1869 Shakespeare Shorts – Language Arts Gr. 4-6
OTM-14181 Sight Words Activities Gr. 1
OTM-299 Simple Machines Gr. 4-6
OTM-2122 Solar System Gr. 4-6
OTM-205 Space Gr. 2-3
OTM-1834 Spelling Blacklines Gr. 1
OTM-1835 Spelling Blacklines Gr. 2
OTM-1814 Spelling Gr. 1
OTM-1815 Spelling Gr. 2
OTM-1816 Spelling Gr. 3
OTM-1817 Spelling Gr. 4
OTM-1818 Spelling Gr. 5
OTM-1819 Spelling Gr. 6
OTM-1827 Spelling Worksavers #1 Gr. 3-5
OTM-2125 Stable Structures & Mechanisms 3
OTM-14139 Stone Fox NS Gr. 4-6
OTM-14214 Stone Orchard NS Gr. 7-8
OTM-1864 Story Starters Gr. 1-3
OTM-1865 Story Starters Gr. 4-6
OTM-1873 Story Starters Gr. 1-6
OTM-2509 Story Writing Gr. 1-3
OTM-2111 Structures, Mechanisms & Motion 2

OTM-14211 Stuart Little NS Gr. 4-6
OTM-1129 Subtraction Drills Gr. 1-3
OTM-2505 Subtraction Gr. 1-3
OTM-2511 Successful Language Pract. Gr. 1-3
OTM-2512 Successful Math Practice Gr. 1-3
OTM-2309 Summer Learning Gr. K-1
OTM-2310 Summer Learning Gr. 1-2
OTM-2311 Summer Learning Gr. 2-3
OTM-2312 Summer Learning Gr. 3-4
OTM-2313 Summer Learning Gr. 4-5
OTM-2314 Summer Learning Gr. 5-6
OTM-14159 Summer of the Swans NS Gr. 4-6
OTM-1418 Superfudge NS Gr. 4-6
OTM-108 Switzerland Gr. 4-6
OTM-115 Take a Trip to Australia Gr. 2-3
OTM-2102 Taking Off With Flight Gr. 1-3
OTM-1455 Tales of the Fourth Grade NS 4-6
OTM-1472 Ticket to Curlew NS Gr. 4-6
OTM-14222 To Kill a Mockingbird NS Gr. 7-8
OTM-14163 Traditional Poetry Gr. 7-10
OTM-1481 Tuck Everlasting NS Gr. 4-6
OTM-14126 Turtles in Literature Gr. 1-3
OTM-1427 Unicorns in Literature Gr. 3-5
OTM-617 Viking Age Gr. 4-6
OTM-14206 War with Grandpa NS Gr. 4-6
OTM-2124 Water Gr. 2-4
OTM-260 Weather Gr. 4-6
OTM-1417 Wee Folk in Literature Gr. 3-5
OTM-808 What is a Community? Gr. 2-4
OTM-262 What is the Weather Today? 2-4
OTM-1473 Where the Red Fern Grows NS 7-8
OTM-1487 Where the Wild Things Are NS 1-3
OTM-14187 Whipping Boy NS Gr. 4-6
OTM-14226 Who is Frances Rain? NS Gr. 4-6
OTM-14213 Wolf Island NS Gr. 1-3
OTM-14221 Wrinkle in Time NS Gr. 7-8